For my sons,

Greg & Jeff

My Bent Tree

by Kathy Brodsky

Illustrations by Cameron Bennett

One day I was walking...

...and was so surprised!!

I spotted a bent pine
beside the straight guys.

I walked right up to it,
I wanted to see...

My eyes never lied.

No tricks played on me!

A booming voice echoed
from way up above.

I heard someone shout out,
"Hello there, my love."

"Who are you?"

I questioned.

"I'm seeing a pine

whose trunk is so crooked.

It's not in a line!"

"I *am* who you see,"
the tree said to me.

"I try to stand tall
and straight as can be.

When I was quite young
a huge lightning bolt
hit me and hurt me.

It gave me a jolt!

I looked weak and skinny.
Mom stayed by my side.

She took care of me
and helped me survive.

Mom helped me get strong.

I could do it all;

though different from others,

I would stand up tall.

Today I'm much stronger
but still somewhat bent.

Sometimes we are fine
in spite of our dents."

I went very often
to visit my pine.

He gave cooling shade
and made me feel fine.

Our woods began changing
when many years passed.

My crooked pine told me,

"This year is my last."

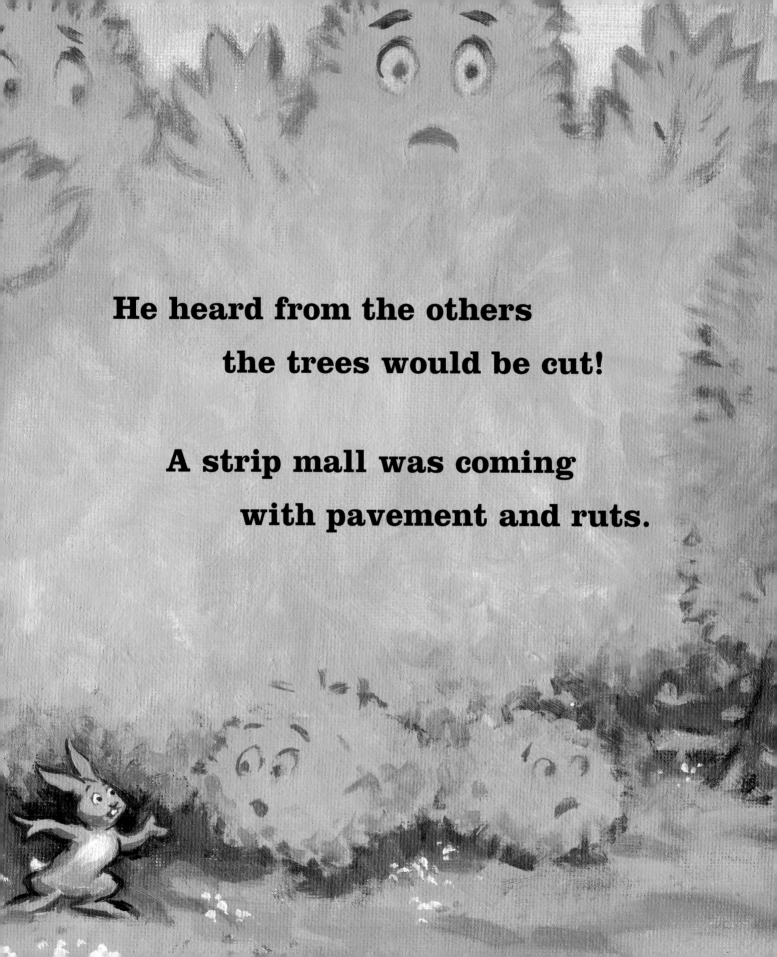

He heard from the others
       the trees would be cut!

A strip mall was coming
       with pavement and ruts.

I couldn't believe it!
Would we lose the woods
that brought so much joy
to the whole neighborhood?

We had to do something!

We worked out a plan.

We all marched together
To save our GREEN land.

We won a GREEN space
with benches and trees...

...where people could visit,
feel calm and at ease.

When I see him these days,
my happy bent pine
is so glad to see me –
he gives the "Hi" sign.

I love my GREEN park surrounding the mall, especially my friend who's TALLEST OF ALL!

My Bent Tree

People

Do you know any people who are different?

   How are they different?

   Can you see what's different?

How would you treat someone who is different?

   Can that person do something you can't?

How are we all the same?

Has anyone helped you to be the strong person you are today?

   Who was that?

   How did they help you?

How can we help ourselves?

How can we help others?

If something is happening that you don't like, what could you do?

How would you begin to make changes?

Discussion Questions for Teachers & Parents about People & Trees

Trees

Is there a tree in front of your house or school?

    What does the tree look like?

    Does it have leaves in winter?

    Do you think the tree is young or old?

    How can you tell?

What do trees do for us?

How do trees help animals?

What would happen if we didn't have shade?

Do you know of a place where there used to be trees but the trees are now gone?

    What happened to them?

If a tree could talk, what do you think it might tell us?

Have you ever hugged a tree?

Additional Questions:

What messages did you find in this story?

What were your favorite parts?

Author's Note

The story of *My Bent Tree* is based on my experience.

One day while walking my dog on our regular route, I looked up and saw a crooked pine. I had never noticed it before. The next day I wrote the first four lines of the poem that eventually became the book *My Bent Tree*.

As I worked on the poem I realized that the crooked pine reminded me of a childhood illness that changed my life.

When I was four years old I had polio. My mother took care of me and nursed me back to health. She encouraged me through many doctors' visits and therapeutic exercises; she helped me to regain my strength and to become the strong person I am today.

As a therapist, a Clinical Social Worker, for almost 40 years, I've worked with many people who have struggled to overcome personal difficulties that started in childhood. Their stories often reveal great courage, inner strength and joy.

From my clients I've gained valuable insights into what people endure on a daily basis. I realized that we are more alike than different and I wanted to help others understand this. That is why I started writing, publishing my first book *Moments in Our Lives* in 2004, and why I created my website helpingwords.com.

I hope that by sharing the story of *My Bent Tree*, people will realize that no matter how hurt or damaged we feel, we all have unique gifts. By reaching out and helping others, we also help ourselves.

Writing *My Bent Tree* has been a wonderful experience for me.

I look forward to hearing from you. Please contact me at:

www.mybenttree.com
or
www.helpingwords.com

Thank you

Kathy Brodsky

Thanks to everyone who helped *My Bent Tree* become a reality –
especially Cameron, Greg, Julia, Louise, Pamme, Bedford writers' group, Aaron and Karen at
Printers Square, and to all of the others who gave help and encouragement.

Publisher's Cataloging-in-Publication
(Provided by Quality Books, Inc.)

Brodsky, Kathy.
    My bent tree / by Kathy Brodsky ; illustrations by
Cameron Bennett.
        p. cm.
    SUMMARY: In this rhyming story, a little girl walking
in the woods befriends a pine tree that is bent. When
construction of a new strip mall means cutting down the
forest, the little girl and others work together to
protect the trees and create a park near the mall.
Includes discussion questions for teachers, parents and
children.
    ISBN-13: 978-0-615-16066-5
    ISBN-10: 0-615-16066-2

    1. Trees--Juvenile fiction. 2. Friendship--Juvenile
fiction. 3. Human ecology--Juvenile fiction. [1. Trees
--Fiction. 2. Friendship--Fiction. 3. Human ecology--
Fiction. 4. Ecology--Fiction. 5. Stories in rhyme.]
I. Bennett, Cameron (Cameron D.), ill. II. Title.

PZ8.3.B782My 2008   [Fic]
                          QBI07-600243

Published by Helpingwords

My Bent Tree © 2008

Printed in the U.S.A.

Printed on recycled paper

For more information contact:

**Kathy Brodsky
Helpingwords
66 Prospect Street
Manchester, NH 03104**

ISBN 978-0-615-16066-5